SIX
GENTLE
CRIMINALS

SIX GENTLE CRIMINALS

Katharine Moore

Allison & Busby
published by W. H. Allen & Co Plc

An Allison & Busby book
Published in 1990 by
W. H. Allen & Co. Plc
Sekforde House
175/9 St John Street
London EC1V 4LL

Copyright © Katharine Moore 1990

Printed in Great Britain by
Bookcraft Ltd, Midsomer Norton, Avon

ISBN 0 85031 845 9

CONTENTS

To
Peter Kingshill
and
Jonathan Fischel

SISTER AGNES

THE BELL OF THE great gate of the Convent sounded and Sister Agnes went to open it. She was old, and shuffled with a curious crablike gait across the wide, black and white tiled hall. A stranger stood in the gateway enquiring for Reverend Mother Elizabeth. She knew who he must be, a friend of Reverend Mother's, who had come to see an old picture that might be sold. Sister Agnes showed him into the salon. Nothing had been changed in the salon for quite a hundred years. There had always been the four upright chairs set at exact intervals round the table that was always covered with a clean white lace-bordered cloth; there was always the giant plant in the window diffusing the dim green light and always the towering crucifix above the grey marble mantelpiece. That was as it should be, but too much had changed since Sister Agnes had come to the convent as a young girl. Ah then it had been such a big prosperous place, like a busy, happy hive of bees, she thought. There was the school in the building at the other end of the garden and the Chapel there, which when she had first seen it she had believed must be one of the most beautiful buildings in the world. Now the school had been closed for years and, because there were so few sisters left in the community, they had converted a room in the main building and used this as a little chapel. Reverend Mother said it was much better than feeling shrunk and lost, but it was so plain and bare, and the new wooden statue of Our Lady that had been given them lately, was so thin and stern.

The presence of the stranger reminded Sister Agnes of all these things which she hated to think of, for she was very much afraid that other and worse changes still might be gathering like a dark cloud. Reverend Mother came bustling into the salon. She was a cheerful and loquacious woman. "It is so good of you to come," she said, "and I am sure you will be able to advise us about our picture. It was here when the old mansion was made over to the church—this part of the Convent goes back to the late 17th century you know, and then in the 19th century it was greatly enlarged and the school and chapel built—all too big for us now I fear, and expenses rising and no new novices coming along, and the latest blow is that we must install elaborate fire precautions or give up our guest rooms, which are such an important source of our income. We cannot really afford to maintain the other building any more, I mean the one where the school and the big Chapel were, and we have had an offer for it from an hotel firm,—not what one would like at all, of course, but things cannot always be as one would like." She paused for breath and James Ellis made sympathetic noises. He was an art historian on his way to a business conference at Antwerp, and he had been asked by Mother Elizabeth, who was an old family friend, to call at the Convent. "Now, about the picture," she went on, "it has been suggested that it may be very valuable, even possibly a Claude. We must not expect miracles, I know, but I think we should do all that we can to make miracles possible, and if indeed it were to turn out to be a Claude, it would go far to solve our problems.''

''It certainly would,'' said Ellis, ''but Claudes are carefully documented, I'm afraid. Anyway let us see.''

The picture hung where it had always hung, above a great chest in the hall. Ellis was not impressed at first sight. It was not in good condition, badly needing cleaning and repair and was a stereotyped classical scene—two solid banks of dark trees, a round moon between, shining upon a Greek temple with nymphs and shepherds dancing in the foreground. There was no signature visible, but one might be lurking in the shadows.

''School of Claude, at any rate, I should say. I'd like to see if I can discover a name, and I'll take a few photos to show a friend of mine in Antwerp, who's an expert on the period. I'd rather not give any judgement as to value before this. I'll call in, if I may, on my way home and tell you what we think.''

He went to fetch what was needed from his car and set to work. Sister Agnes, whose business it was to answer the door that day, passed through the hall several times and watched him. At the end of the morning, when he had finished his examination, she went up to him and touched him on the arm. ''I can show you much more beautiful pictures than that; clear, bright, holy pictures,'' said Sister Agnes. ''Come.'' It was less an invitation than a command and Ellis, intrigued, followed her obediently. They went across the hall into a garden with long, formal beds and a straight path leading to the disused school buildings. Sister Agnes always kept a key to this building under a certain ledge, for Reverend Mother allowed her access whenever she wished. She led Ellis down an empty corridor lined on each side with many shut, silent doors—then she opened a larger door beneath an archway and ushered him into what seemed at first to be a brilliantly-lit interior filled with people; light streamed in from the crudely coloured stained glass windows and life-size painted figures jostled one another upon the walls. There was a profusion of carved wood and embroidered hangings and brass candlesticks.

Sister Agnes waited expectantly. "They were done by Sister Dorothy," she said. "She was my teacher when I was at school here. They are the story of her own name Saint, Dorothea. See, there are her red roses and golden apples. When I saw them first they looked just as they do now, they have never faded. Are not the colours most lovely? Are these not marvellous pictures?"

"They are certainly fine," said James Ellis. To himself he said, "One must admit there is something to admire in the self-confidence that can paint on such a scale, whatever the results."

"And the Chapel," said Sister Agnes, "it is so beautiful and now it is never, never used."

"Well," said Ellis, looking round, "it certainly doesn't look neglected."

"I am permitted to care for it by Reverend Mother," she said with pride. "Our Lady has as lovely flowers here and as fresh as in the other Chapel and I light candles for her here on her feastdays, and here she smiles always—there, in the little Chapel she is stern and sad."

The vapid, sweet face of the large marble Madonna

14

near the altar, stared down at them. She wore a gauzy spangled muslin robe. Sister Agnes gently re-arranged its folds. "He cannot have seen many places more beautiful than this," she thought, "he is struck silent."

Ellis was in fact feeling that his response had been inadequate. He said now as warmly as he could, "These paintings are in excellent condition, no signs of damp or decay."

"When it is very wet I light an oil stove," said Sister Agnes, "there is no central heating in this building."

"Much better for pictures," said Ellis and he added, "I wonder what will happen to them if the place has to be sold."

There was a silence. Then, "Happen to them? Sold?" whispered Sister Agnes.

He looked at her in dismay. Surely, he thought, Mother Elizabeth had talked as if the troubles of the Convent were common knowledge. "I beg your pardon," he said, "if I've said anything to worry you,—it's been rumoured, that's all."

"Then they were false rumours," said Sister Agnes. "wicked rumours." She still whispered as if to speak aloud such things in the Chapel was a sacrilege, but even as she spoke she knew that they were true. Up to now she had closed her ears resolutely to all this talk about money and the need for it. She had not even allowed herself to pray for help, for that would be to admit fear. But the clouds had gathered on the horizon and now here was this man, this inhabitant of that strange, alien, frightening world outside the Convent gates talking to her so casually, so certainly, of the unspeakable. And at his words the cloud had come close and enveloped her. She turned without another word and led the way out of the Chapel. But the old picture—she hadn't thought much before about this business of the old, ugly picture, but now, as they re-entered the hall where it hung, she stopped suddenly and said:

"You will sell the picture for us? Reverend Mother says so, and that will save us?"

Ellis could not resist her imploring gaze.

"Don't be distressed, please, I will do my best," he said.

Some days later he was back at the Convent and again it was Sister Agnes who let him in. She fumbled with the refastening of the gate in her anxiety, but there was no chance to question him, for Reverend Mother was crossing the hall to greet him and they disappeared together into her office. It was evening, the hour before compline, usually a placid and peaceful time, but today Sister Agnes could not be at peace. She went to walk in the garden to calm herself, but it was not long before Mother Elizabeth called all the community together. She told them that there was no very good news. The picture was not so valuable as had been hoped—it had been identified by Mr Ellis and his friend as the work of an imitator of Claude—a mediocre painter, not highly thought of or sought after and, because of this and its poor condition, not worth more than about ten thousand francs. "So we must do without our miracle," she said, "and the sale of the school building and the Chapel must, I fear, go forward, for it is only thus that we will be enabled to continue our life of service and of praise together in this place. This we must now accept as Our Lord's will."

Sister Agnes crept up to her room after compline was

over. She knelt before her window, which looked out over the clustering roofs to the soaring spire of Our Lady's great church. She could not believe that Reverend Mother was right. It could not be Our Lord's will that His House should be destroyed or, even worse, desecrated; put to what purpose? A hotel would not want a chapel. What then, a restaurant? A concert hall? "No, no," she repeated passionately to herself. Perhaps it had been wrong to look for deliverance from that pagan picture—she could understand that, but now another way out *must* be found and perhaps it was she and she alone who was called to find it.

The words of the child, Samuel, came to her. "Speak Lord, for thy servant heareth." He was weak and helpless yet Our Lord used him. She closed her eyes in prayer. When she opened them again the lime trees in the little square below the window were gold and black in the setting sun, but the great brick spire of the Church was glowing like an immense rose-coloured flame. Sister Agnes gazed and gazed long after it had faded; she was in a trance, both of fear and exaltation, for her prayer had been answered. Our Lady's Church had shown her what she must do.

Mother Elizabeth had pressed Ellis to stay over the night at the Convent. "We are still allowed to put up our friends," she said with a smile, "and it is the least we can do after the trouble you have taken." "To no satisfactory end, I fear," said Ellis, but he did not need to get back to London that night and was glad of the quiet guest room overlooking the garden. It was some while after the nuns had all retired that he laid aside his book and his papers and, at length, drew back his curtains. Looking out, he thought he saw in the moonlight a figure flitting down the path. It vanished quickly in the shadows, but not before it had struck him as vaguely familiar. Where had he noticed that odd gait before? A curious hour anyway for one of the Sisters to be out and about. But it was no affair of his; he dismissed the matter and went to sleep.

Sister Agnes let herself into the Chapel, which the silver light of the moon had changed into the place of exquisite loveliness that, for her, it had always been. The frescoes gleamed with a transforming radiance, the face of the smiling Madonna above her pale flowers, was moulded into unearthly beauty. It seemed to Sister Agnes that everything had been awaiting her and was now welcoming her in expectation. She knelt for a time in prayer. When she rose from her knees the moonlight had disappeared and all was dark, but she did not need to see to find her way to the cupboard where she kept oil and matches and a store of candles. She lit a taper and with it she lit first the candles on the Altar, then the great candle that was set at one side of the Virgin's statue. Next she filled up the stove and dragged it from its place beside the cupboard door all the way up the aisle, and then propped it against the screen; it left a trail of oil in its wake. Then she fetched more candles and stuck them in the sconces of the choir stalls. "Not for long, so very long, will there have been such a glory here as I shall make tonight," said Sister Agnes. She no longer felt afraid. She fetched out the last of her store of candles and lit them also and, holding as many as she could grasp with both hands, she held them high above her head. "O ye fire and heat, bless ye the Lord. Praise Him and Magnify Him forever," cried Sister Agnes. Then she hurled her bright bunch of flames at the Virgin's feet and went from the building.

The alarm was not given till hours afterwards. James Ellis woke to the sound of the convent bell clanging vigorously, to a roaring noise and a great glow in the sky. He sprang to the window. Beneath him a crowd of little black figures were outlined against a backcloth of fire—"like a medieval painting," Ellis thought. He snatched up a coat and ran downstairs and into the garden where Mother Elizabeth was trying to calm her flock. "There is no danger to us, see the wind is blowing the flames quite the other way. The engines will be here directly. Ah, here they come." But they were not in time to save the Chapel or much of the adjoining building, for the fire had gained too much ground during the night. The little crowd continued to watch spellbound as the firemen gradually subdued the flames. It was a chilly dawn and Ellis, as soon as he saw that no help was needed, went back into the house to dress. It appeared silent and deserted but, mounting the stairs, he thought he heard a slight noise and, looking up, he saw a small solitary figure motionless at the landing window above him. She turned as he came on towards her and he saw it was the old nun who had let him into the convent and had shown him the terrible frescoes. "This must be dreadful for you," he exclaimed, "your chapel—I am so very sorry."

She looked at him calmly. "It is Our Lord's will," she said, and smiled, and then shuffled slowly away down the passage.

By breakfast time there was only a smouldering ruin left and life was resuming its normal orderly course at the Convent. As to the cause of the fire, this was thought to be a fault in the electric wiring. "I blame myself," said Mother Elizabeth. "It is old and I should have known it was due for an overhaul when we put in our heating here."

Ellis left for home that day, promising to arrange for the sale of the picture should she think it worthwhile.

Some weeks later he heard from her. "The Insurance people have paid up handsomely," she wrote, "so that no sale of the site will be necessary, let alone of the picture. You see, I am right to believe in miracles and we are to have ours after all. The ruins have been cleared and we are making a garden where the Chapel stood. Do you remember dear old Sister Agnes? The statue of Our Lady which stood in the Chapel has been recovered and was not much damaged by the fire. It is to be set up in the new garden and the roses we are going to plant round it are to be Sister Agnes's special care."

Yes, he remembered Sister Agnes very well. He had not, at the time, thought it necessary to mention to anyone that moonlit figure making for the Chapel on the night of the fire, nor did he think to do so now. He had no proof whatever, although, together with that odd encounter on the landing, he felt there was something here he did not understand. But Sister Agnes and arson! the idea was preposterous—she had probably never heard of such a thing, besides she had loved the Chapel so ardently. It must, he decided, remain a mystery, for now everyone was happy, except perhaps the Insurance people, but they, he was sure, could bear the loss with equanimity.

THE ROMANTIC

WILFRED SUGDEN WAS not the sort of man you would suspect of being a romantic. He certainly never suspected it of himself. In appearance he did not attract a second glance. He was close on middle age, had thin, mouse-coloured hair, pale grey eyes, a little moustache and a slightly receding chin. He was not well off and held a modest post in a Bank. He lived by himself in a small, neat flat near Earls Court. He was the sort of man who always sat on the edge of chairs. He had had no love life at all, though once he had nearly proposed to a girl. She travelled into the City every day by the same tube train as himself and she had wonderful hair, real corn-coloured (you could easily see it wasn't dyed) and big brown eyes and a crooked smile, and in time he plucked up enough courage to talk to her about the weather and then to ask her name, which was Isobel and at last to date her for a film. After that he began to think about her constantly. They went out together two Saturdays (it was spring), first to Kensington Gardens and then to Kew, and then the next Saturday she asked him to come back with her to supper. She too lived alone, she had told him, and had a job in a publishing firm. On the way to her flat, which was in South Kensington, quite a good part, Wilfred felt that those eyes and that hair were getting too much for him. Afterwards he knew that if they had been going to his flat instead, or anywhere in fact but where they did

23

go, he would have asked her to marry him and "then what would I have let myself in for?" He didn't like to think, for when she led him into her sitting room, through a passage blocked up with a pile of old coats and a cat basket, you could hardly see the carpet for books and boots and mugs and a dirty saucepan. The table was piled with papers and unwashed dishes with a large tabby cat busily licking them and a jug of half-dead flowers and an ironing board, and there wasn't an empty chair anywhere. Isobel didn't seem to mind the mess at all. She just swept a space clear on the table and the nearest seat and said, "Make yourself at home while I see if Maximus has left anything for us to eat." She went into the kitchen and the cat followed her. Wilfred was one of those people for whom animals don't exist except as nuisances. He couldn't accept a cat called Maximus, licking everywhere and everything, and he hated disorder. He shuddered. When Isobel at length emerged, carrying a tray, he ate and drank as little as he could and went away as soon as he could. He left very upset, but his own flat welcomed and enfolded him with its shining shelves, its symmetrically arranged furniture and rugs, its spotless china, and he saw that it was no use—it would never do. He felt relieved but sad on the whole, though the relief was greater than the regret. For a week he went to work by bus, but it took too long so he made up his mind to catch his usual train again and she was there, but seemed to be avoiding him and they just nodded at each other and after a while he didn't see her any more.

Wilfred quite liked his work—for the rest he did his own cleaning and cooking, and this took up a lot of

time as his standards were high. He had a friend, a
fellow clerk, with whom he played chess, but he had
very few relatives as he was an only child of only
children—fecundity not being a characteristic of the
family. He had a second cousin however, whom he
was in the habit of visiting regularly. Arthur Sugden
was a widower who lived in a rambling old house in
the Chilterns. He was something of an invalid and had
a housekeeper companion called Mrs Allen, and when
Mrs Allen took a holiday Wilfred was in request.

Although he knew his cousin was just making use
of him and rather despised him, Wilfred liked going
to 'The Homestead'. His duties there were not onerous
and it was a cut above his usual surroundings; this
appealed to the snob in him and he enjoyed the luxury
of good wine and food for the gardener's wife came
in to cook and she had a natural gift. But Wilfred was
also aware of a sense of satisfaction which the solid,
well-kept furniture and the many pictures gave him.
These last were actually rather special, for Arthur
Sugden's father had had an eye for pictures. His little
collection of 19th century paintings were hung in the
morning room through which Wilfred had to pass to
reach the staircase that led to the bedroom he always
occupied, and he generally paused to look at them as
he went to and fro. They gave him a faint but definite
pleasure. They were mostly water colours, but there
was a large oil seascape and a smaller figure oil painting
of a girl looking out of a window. Since his abortive
affair, Wilfred had taken particular note of this picture.
The girl was turned three-quarters away from the
viewer, so that only a fraction of her face was visible,
but there was something in her pose that reminded

him strongly of Isobel and the hair was very like. The room in which she stood was cool and softly lit, and commendably empty of all but a small table with a sedate blue and white bowl upon it. All the light in the picture was concentrated on the girl's hair, which reflected the gilt of the rather beautiful frame. It was a charming little picture, and each time Wilfred went to the Homestead he felt its fascination grow stronger and, as the impression of the real Isobel faded, so he came gradually to identify the ideal Isobel with the girl in the picture.

Arthur Sugden did not care much about the paintings. They would go with the rest of the property to an only son farming in Australia who cared even less. "Alec will sell the old place, of course," said his father, "but I shall be beyond caring. Those pictures ought to bring in something—they tell me Victorians are coming into fashion again—that girl by the window, saw the artist mentioned in a sale in *The Times* lately, going for quite a decent sum—can't remember the name of the fellow—saw you looking at it the other day. What *is* the name?" Wilfred didn't know: the artist did not interest him, only the picture. He found he did not at all relish the idea of the paintings being sold. He had never liked Alec, but this was not because he grudged him his inheritance, for he had no expectations from his cousin or no substantial ones, though he had sometimes thought, from hints, that he might come in for some small remembrance, but the hints were too vague for him to bank on this. "Suppose I ought to get them re-insured," went on his cousin: "These burglars are up to anything nowadays, don't know what the police think they're doing, drive about in cars all the time, never see one, hasn't been a policeman in the village for years."

"Perhaps you should get a burglar alarm," suggested Wilfred. "No, no," said Arthur, "dreadful things, always going off by mistake and frightening the life out of you. No, Bonny's worth a dozen of them."

Bonny was the elderly spaniel, in whom Arthur had a touching and quite unjustifiable trust. She barked furiously at the milkman and at Wilfred, but at no-one else. It was one of Wilfred's less attractive duties to take Bonny for walks, which she hated. After this conversation, however, Bonny's basket was moved from the kitchen to an alcove under the stairs next to the morning room.

It was on his next visit that Wilfred, who was a light sleeper, was woken by a curious noise in the passage— a crunching sort of noise. He put on his dressing gown and opened the door. Just outside on the mat Bonny was lying, devouring a large bone. She growled at Wilfred and at once there was another sound from below, a slight scurrying noise. Wilfred stepped over Bonny and descended the stairs. There was a faint light coming from under the morning room door. He stood still, listening, and then heard the sound of a car near at hand, but retreating rapidly in the distance. He turned the handle of the door gently and went in. The light was shining from the porch lamp that was kept alight all night—it was shining through the window that was wide open, the curtain blowing free. It was light enough to see chairs pushed aside and blank spaces on the walls. Two water colours were missing from above the mantelpiece and the big seascape had been removed from its frame, but to Wilfred's relief the "Girl at the Window" was in its place. He advanced into the room and his foot struck an object on the floor—it was a small knife.

What happened next appeared afterwards to him like a dream. Perhaps, indeed, he had supposed himself to be in a dream. He picked up the knife, went towards the portrait of Isobel, neatly cut it all round (the knife was very sharp), ran upstairs with it and laid it and the knife at the bottom of his suitcase. Then he went to rouse his cousin who slept in another wing, and to call the police. Bonny, who had finished her lovely bribe, accompanied him, thinking there still might be unexpected pickings around.

Arthur was not much agitated. "Re-insured all these pictures only last month," he chuckled. "Gave Bonny a bone, did they? She couldn't very well bite them after that, could she? Showed her sense though in getting out of their way and rousing you. Couldn't expect more of the old girl. You look like Father Christmas in that awful hairy red dressing gown Wilfred, better get something decent on before the police arrive. What did you say the rascals took? The seascape and the girl at the window, and the two best landscapes, eh? Knew their stuff, didn't they! Well, we'll see whether the police'll let them get away with them. It's a good thing about the insurance though, isn't it?"

"A very good thing," said Wilfred.

Mrs Allen returned two days later; by then they had heard nothing of the missing pictures. When Wilfred made his departure his cousin said: "I'll keep you in touch,—pity you weren't quicker on the mark, would've been something for you to remember, could have dined out on it and that sort of thing. Still you did your best I've no doubt. Been a bit of a shock, hasn't it, noticed you've not opened your mouth much since.''

When Wilfred got home to his flat he unpacked, emptied a drawer in his bureau and laid the canvas tenderly in it. As he locked the drawer he said solemnly: "I am a thief," but he said it quite without conviction; it did not seem to him possible nor did he feel either regret or compunction—quite the reverse. It was just something that had happened. But it *had* happened and every evening when he got home from work he unlocked the drawer and took out the picture and gazed at it with pleasure. "I shan't keep you hidden forever," he whispered, "just for a time."

He heard from his cousin not long after: "Dear Wilfred, You'll be glad to learn that the police have actually succeeded in tracing three of the pictures. The one that's still missing is that one by that chap whose name I can never remember—you liked it rather I recollect, still it may turn up." Wilfred was a little worried at this news. Somehow he never expected stolen goods to be found again except in fiction. He would have preferred the pictures to have all remained missing. "However," he told himself, "the hue and cry will soon be over—before my next visit to the Homestead anyway." But he did not look forward to this visit with his wonted pleasant anticipation. In the event though, there was to be no visit, or at least not of the usual kind, for about a month before it was due he received another letter, not this time from his cousin but from Mrs Allen saying that Arthur Sugden had died of heart failure, peacefully in his sleep.

Wilfred went down for the funeral. He had not really

been fond of Arthur, but he would miss him. He was someone he had always known and to whom he had been bound by those family ties of which he had so few and he was quite sad to think he would never be going to the old place again. He had, however, a small hopeful expectation; perhaps after all there would be some legacy, enough to pay for a rather luxurious holiday somewhere. But there was no mention of Wilfred at all in the Will and Alec, the son, over from his Australian farm, was very much in charge, already talking obnoxiously of a sale of the house and all its contents. Before Wilfred left, however, Alec handed over to him a square package. It was labelled "For Wilfred Sugden" in his cousin's handwriting with a date, the date of his last visit.

It was a wooden case which, when he got home, Wilfred had to open carefully with a hammer. Inside were shavings and from these he drew out a picture frame. He recognized it at once as the frame belonging to 'the girl at the window'. "So he knew all the time!" exclaimed Wilfred incredulously, and his first feeling was of affront. How dared his cousin imagine such a thing! "Why I myself would never have thought it. How could he have guessed? I don't see how he could have known." He stood staring down at the frame and as he stared his eyes caught a flicker of scarlet against the gilt of one corner. "So that was it," he thought peering at it, "and that hair probably cost me my legacy—well, fair enough." He took the frame to the drawer of the bureau and laid it gently over the picture. "It was well worth it," he said, "where might you have landed up? I would never have seen you again Isobel." He reframed her himself later; he was quite competent

30

with tools and he thought it safer than trusting her to a shop. His friend Higgins came to play chess the evening after he had hung Isobel over the bureau. "I've got a new picture," Wilfred said. "Oh yes," said Higgins, throwing it a glance, "nice frame, don't like not seeing the girl's face though, looks as if she might be a stunner . . . you've lost your castle."

As time went on Wilfred might be said to have become a little eccentric, as people may do when they live alone. He fell into the habit of talking regularly to his picture every evening, telling it all that had happened to him during the day. He had often before thought that it would be delightful to have someone to whom he could do this. The girl in the picture always listened attentively, she was always there when he wanted her, always peaceful and composed, and the room in which she stood always as he had left it, and as it ought to be. It did not trouble him at all that her back was towards him. He knew he had only to wait and if one waits, presumably there is something to wait for. One day he knew she would turn and look at him with her large brown eyes and smile at him—he remembered her crooked smile very well. Yes, she would turn, and then? Meanwhile he was quite content—perhaps indeed waiting was best.

BETHESDA HOUSE

MAJOR RICHARD RADCLIFFE, in default of
other heirs, had come in for a property in
Northamptonshire. It had belonged to his
uncle—an old recluse who had taken a long while to
die. The Major had only met him once long ago as a
boy when they had both heartily disliked each other,
so there was no grief at the news of his death. Dickie
remembered rather hating his uncle's home, which was
a large forbidding-looking Victorian mansion backed
by a dark fir wood with a small pond at its verge. "If
only it had been a different sort of place," sighed the
Major, "but I'm afraid it's nothing but a white
elephant." He and his wife had been to look at the
house and it had more than justified his gloomy
memories. It was about a hundred years old with an
exterior of peeling grey stucco. It faced north and there
were plenty of signs of damp. There was a wide weedy
gravel sweep in front and behind a plot of rough grass,
and then the enclosing wall of fir trees and the pond.

"It won't sell," said the Major, "too remote, too big,
too decayed, too everything—what on earth are we to
do with it?"

"I'll think of something," said Truda.

The Major was a man of few ideas and admired his
wife, who had an abundance of them. However, he
was at first pretty dubious about her really big idea,
which she produced the next morning while they were
at breakfast.

"We must live there," she said decidedly as she poured his coffee. "Now listen, we've got to live somewhere and we've got to live on something; we can't possibly live on your pension alone." The Major had just been retired and as they had lately come back from service abroad, and possessed no settled home, they were at present occupying rather uncomfortable temporary quarters in a friend's flat in Hackney.

"We must live at Rosemount, which is not going to be a white elephant but, on the contrary—a godsend. We must run it as a guest house."

"But no-one is going to want to be a guest in that godforsaken hole," said the Major. "There's nothing whatever for it—besides there's no access—there's a motorway extension planned I believe, about a couple of miles away, but that'll be years ahead."

"Ah!" said Truda, "but this isn't going to be just an ordinary guest house, Dickie, it's to be a Health and Healing Guest House. I thought it all out in bed last night. I knew I should think of something."

The Major snorted loudly.

"Don't do that, dear," said Truda, "just listen quietly. "The thing is to turn all the place's defects into assets—it's easy once you begin."

Truda was at first sight a deceptively plain woman, small with smudgy features and colourless hair, but she could flare into sudden vitality when the rather big greenish eyes behind her spectacles would widen and sparkle. They did so now. "Don't you see, Rosemount is not isolated—it's peaceful. Its north aspect is peculiarly healthy. Everyone used to know this and built their houses accordingly. It's only fairly

36

recently that there's been this craze for sun. Now people are beginning to realize how dangerous that can be—I read about it only the other day. Bethesda House will be full of lovely cool, cool calm.''

''Bethesda House?'' said the Major, bemused.

''Yes I thought of that in my bath this morning, because of the pool, healing you know—though I don't suppose you will know because you were never brought up properly. Rosemount is such a silly name—there's no mount anyway and no roses, though granted we could plant some, but I don't think we will, it would spoil the view.''

''There isn't one to spoil,'' said the Major.

''That's just it,'' said Truda triumphantly, ''no distraction, just green thoughts in a green shade—oh we can do a lot with that marvellous forest.''

''When does a wood become a forest?'' thought the Major. ''It's a point I don't really know.''

Truda recalled his attention by suddenly chanting: ''You are nearer God's heart in a forest than anywhere else on earth.''

''It's garden, not forest,'' he said, for he wasn't wholly illiterate.

''I know that perfectly well,'' said Truda, ''but anyone can have a garden—we, at Bethesda House, have got a forest. We'll call all the rooms after trees—we could have a picture in each; all that wonderful growth—so healthy! And the sap!''

''The sap,'' repeated the Major, stupefied.

''Oh Dick,'' and Truda's eyes were now quite brilliant, ''I've got such a good idea about the sap. It's not much use nowadays just having a diet, they've all been used up—no fat, no meat, no starch, no sugar, no coffee, no milk—or nothing but milk, nothing but starch—nothing at all. Oh there's no end to them and they're all stale,—though nothing at all is perhaps a good idea for the first day or two, it must save the housekeeping bills. But Bethesda House must offer something new, something special, and it could be an Elixir, golden bottles of it, very, very expensive,'' said Truda happily, ''brewed each year when the sap is rising.''

''But what will it be made of?'' asked the Major, ''you don't know how to tap trees,—besides, you might poison people.''

''Oh it doesn't matter what it's made of,'' said Truda, ''it's the association—new life, nature, everyone knows that nature is healthy. Of course, though, the elixir won't be enough on its own.''

But it was enough for the Major at present, and he said it was time he took the hound out for his morning walk. The hound, a fat, pleasant retriever called Winston, obviously didn't fancy a walk that morning, but knew he was going to have one and followed the Major from the room very, very slowly.

Truda went on elaborating her big idea at intervals all through the day.

''I shall give psychiatric treatment,'' she said at lunch.

''But you can't, Truda, you don't know how and besides you haven't any qualifications.''

''Of course I know how—anyone could if they gave their mind to it, even you could, Dick, it's much easier than bridge, and a few letters after your name is cheaper than a bottle of whisky I should think; well perhaps than a case, we shall see.''

At tea time she said, "I think I can manage healing hands."

"But your hands aren't healing."

"How do you know, dear?" She looked at them speculatively and thought, not for the first time, that they were rather nice hands. So did the Major, but he said dubiously, "Don't you have to be religious for that sort of thing?"

"Not really, not nowadays," said Truda, "perhaps a tiny bit Eastern—a touch here and there. I won't overdo it—it's the association that matters."

Truda had her practical side. At supper she said: "Domestic help—your uncle must have had some, but you wouldn't know about that, Dick, would you?"

The Major shook his head.

"There must be some available in the village," said Truda, "it's such an old world place, and it would be a good idea, don't you think, to encourage some of our guests to do their part, just making their own beds, setting the tables and doing the flowers, that sort of thing—perhaps a little dusting and washing-up, though we must get a machine, I suppose. But when you've been laid aside as it were, it is such a joy to feel of use. I shall call them 'busy bees', I think." She began to hum 'Land of Hope and Glory', always a sign of triumph.

"You won't take in anyone really ill, will you, Truda?" said the Major uneasily—"you might kill them." He had already sadly accepted the probability that Bethesda House would actually materialize.

And of course it did. Faith, as everyone knows, can move mountains, let alone such small matters as reconditioning an old house. Truda had unlimited faith in herself and the Major in her, and with her energy and his patient toil, great progress was made in a short time.

Truda had more and more ideas. She unearthed a most useful young art student, a distant cousin of Dick's, who was persuaded that it would be excellent practice, perhaps leading to commissions, to spend her vacation painting garlands of oak, ash and thorn or whatever the appropriate tree might be, over the doors of each of the guest rooms, and a splendid tree of heaven in the hall. Truda's own room, the one in which she intended to hold her healing sessions, was all in different harmonious shades of green, with an enchanting gold zodiac in the ceiling. The art student also designed two overalls for her—one of interlacing leaves, the other of a waving silvery pattern, like the pool on a windy fine day. The change from one to the other overall was to be highly significant for the patient, Truda explained to the Major.

Everything was ready for the first arrivals before a year was out. The Major still disliked the house, but was reconciled to the forest and the pool because Winston approved of them. Being a retriever, he liked wallowing in water, and the pine trees had a rejuvenating effect on him, as indeed, fortunately, it seemed also to have on the guests, and pretty soon Bethesda House began to prove a going concern.

They were lucky from the first. Truda took care to advertise in the right sort of periodicals—the sort that had never come the Major's way before. How she ever got to know about them astonished him. But it was he who was responsible for their very first guest, who gave them a flying start. They had been discussing

possible contacts; Truda, who was in her practical
mood, said: "They mustn't know us very well, you
see that, don't you, Dick?"

The Major nodded decisively. "What about that
American fellow and his wife we met in Germany on
our last trip there? They didn't have time to know us
hardly at all, but she took a fancy to you, Truda. I
remember that because I was always being landed with
him on my own."

"Abby Buckwhistle!" exclaimed Truda, "she gave
me her address, and I've kept it in case we landed up
one day in the States."

And it actually turned out that Abby had a dear
friend exiled in England who hadn't been able to match
up with the right psychiatrist yet. The American
contact, thus quickly established, proved steadily
productive, and the home supply, though slower to
start, grew rapidly.

"You must try Bethesda House, darling, it has done
wonders for Lady Quinton. Dr Truda Radcliffe is a
marvel she says, and she is never without Dr Truda's
special elixir."

"What I said to my husband is that it's worth any
money to find someone who really cares," said old Mrs
Harbottle; "Dr Radcliffe never spares herself."

As a matter of fact Truda, though she worked hard,
was very happy; she had always been successful in
amateur theatricals, and now she was even more
successful. She enjoyed the sessions with her patients.
She had a clear, flexible voice and it sounded many
various notes ranging from the tender and cajoling to
delightful sternness and bullying. It made the Major
chuckle whenever he chanced to overhear it. "She

sounds just like one of those TV advertising chumps,''
he thought proudly.

He himself was more than reconciled to the state of
affairs. At first he had woken sometimes from sleep
to see the words 'committed for FRAUD' written in
green letters against the blackness of the night, or to
hear an imaginary fatal groan from the nearest guest
room but, as time passed, his steadily growing bank
balance could not but be comforting, for by the
beginning of their third year at Bethesda House there
was a waiting list, and Truda did not seem to have done
any harm; in fact he was coming to the conclusion that
she did good. After all she had always done *him* good.
Also, there was no denying it, he sometimes found
some of the guests entertaining.

"Mrs Bellamy has brought a niece with her this
time,'' said Truda one day. "She's quite young and
rather like a dryad, I think.''

"What's a dryad?'' asked the Major.

"A wood nymph, dear,'' said Truda.

"Oh, is she a beauty then?''

"Dryads don't have to be beautiful, exactly.''

"Attractive though?''

"Yes—definitely.''

"D'you know what you remind me of?'' the Major
asked the girl later that same day. She looked up at
him with large, brown eyes rather too heavily made
up, and blinked them rapidly.

"*Do* tell me,'' she said.

"A dryad,'' said the Major, adding boldly, "and
dryads like woods, you know. Will you come for a walk
with Winston and me in our wood?''

The walk was a success. "I do think the Major is a

sweetie,'' said the dryad to her aunt, and repeated that
sentiment with variations during the rest of her visit.

After the dryad was the witch. ''Ah,'' said Truda,
reading from a letter she had received that morning,
''a new applicant. Quite a good address and
recommended by Lady Quinton, sounds promising,
suffers from severe nervous prostrations. Oh dear, we
must certainly do what we can for her.''

''I've seen her already,'' said the Major
unexpectedly, ''she was spying out the place last week
when you were out.''

''How do you know it was her?''

''I didn't, but it must have been—actually she's quite
noticeable. She struck me as rather like a witch.''

''Oh, is she very ugly then?''

''No,'' said the Major reflectively, ''not yet. Mouth
and nose already a bit too close though, but good eyes
and hair.

''Witches don't always have to be ugly,'' he added.

''Don't they?'' said Truda.

''Definitely not,'' said the Major.

Witches are also at home in a wood, and the Major
and Winston and the witch spent quite a lot of time
there during her stay at Bethesda House. She went,
after having paid a sizeable bill, but then, when she
left, no one would ever have supposed her to have
suffered from her nerves, though she booked in for
another session quite soon.

''I really must add you to our brochure, Dick,'' said
Truda, ''you're such an asset!''

The more elderly guests tended to form two groups
as regards their attitude towards the Major and Truda.
Some, for instance, (this was during the witch's visit)

agreed that a word dropped into someone's ear was advisable, the only question being whose ear and who was to drop it. "Of course one doesn't want to make mischief," said Lady Quinton, "but on the other hand is it quite fair to dear Dr Truda not to give just the hint of a warning?" But others held that though she could never be accused of neglecting her patients, Truda did sometimes neglect the dear Major, just a little. A man does need to be able to count on his wife for companionship and cosseting when needed.

Lady Quinton was embroidering a cushion cover for Truda's birthday—"It's not till next month, but I'm afraid I'm a slow worker and as it must be a surprise I can't do it when the Doctor is with us."

"Oh," said Mrs Harbottle, "that accounts for it, if she's a Taurus."

"What accounts for what?"

"The Major is Aquarius—and they don't tend to mix very well, that's all. I'm an Aquarius myself, so I know, but of course such difficulties can be overcome. But it calls for sympathy and true understanding."

"Mrs Harbottle keeps patting me whenever I go near her, as if I were Winston," complained the Major to Truda.

Both camps might have been equally surprised and annoyed, had they known with what amusement they were discussed by Truda and the Major over their night drinks, which were, by the way, decidedly not from the Bethesda House elixir.

"Poor dears," said Truda, "gossip is good for them; they need it quite as much as healing hands. We're doing pretty well, Dickie, I think we might afford a holiday soon."

Bethesda House

The Major was pleased at this prospect. It was their third summer without one and he was feeling the heat, for the season was sultry and this kind of weather did not agree with him. Actually this was largely because he had a shameful and inexplicable fear of thunderstorms. He was an averagely brave man (though he had never yet had to be particularly brave) and he was naturally both mortified and secretive about this weakness although, after all, most people have their pet phobias—spiders or caves or burglars. With the Major it happened to be thunderstorms.

On his honeymoon there had been a storm one night, and he had risen hastily to shut the windows and draw the curtains. Truda had said: "You needn't have bothered, Dickie, did you think I'd be scared, you funny boy? Fancy a soldier's wife being frightened of a thunderstorm!" After that, of course, he couldn't confess. Since Truda had taken up with this psychology business he'd sometimes supposed he had been terrified of a storm when a baby. Apparently you never got over things that happened to you as a baby, which made it a bit better because you couldn't be blamed. But there it was—thunder was worse than guns, and lightning was worse still. But he had managed to repress his terror, though it was hard work and even Truda, though she knew storms made him feel queer, never guessed *how* queer.

He was too ashamed of this weakness to think much about it; one need not really think about thunderstorms unless they are actually happening, or when very occasionally they might be mentioned in the media as doing some especial damage to buildings or to people—these always seemed to catch his eye.

One afternoon, not long after the chat about the gossiping guests, the Major decided to seek the shade of the fir trees. The atmosphere was a bit heavy, but the sky seemed clear enough and he whistled to Winston and set out. Truda had her busy bees well organized by this time and one of them was assiduously watering the flower bed, for *one* border had after all been allowed to provide for vases in the house, so many of the guests apparently being keen on flower arrangement. The Major skirted the flower bed rapidly to avoid her, as he knew he should also be busy, the grass needed cutting, but it was too hot for this and he plunged with relief into the wood. The crowded trees stood very still and silent on either side and he wandered on and on along the little paths, pleasantly haunted by memories of dryads and witches. Presently he sat down to rest with his back against a tree trunk, Winston panting at his feet, and soon both were fast asleep.

They woke some time later to a loud burst of thunder. The Major sprang up in terror, then came a brilliant flash of lightning and another deafening clap just overhead. He started forward, stumbled over the dog and fell headlong to the ground. He did not realize that it was Winston that had caused his fall and lay there face downwards in the dark undergrowth. "I've been struck," he said to himself in an overwhelming panic. "That's what's happened."

Truda had hardly noticed the sudden storm; she was too busy with her correspondence. Bookings had fallen off a little for the autumn. Of course people usually began to get ready for their cruises then, but there had been two cancellations, Sonia Smith's tiresome husband had cavilled at her last bill and Auberon Price was joining a brotherhood in California. Then there was the letter she had to write to a Miss Powell who, she had just discovered, had some connection with the BBC. Truda did not much care for such a recommendation and decided to say that she was full up at the time required. "You can't be too careful," said Truda to herself, as she addressed the envelope and firmly stamped it just as Winston bumbled against the French window barking urgently. It was raining quite hard now and, as she let him in, she wondered where Dick was and stood looking out for him across the lawn. She saw him then emerging from the trees, but not directly towards the house. He was taking a curious zig-zag route, with his arms oddly outstretched before him. "He looks as if he were drunk," she thought, but it was seldom that Dick forgot himself and anyway never at this time of the day. "Dickie, Dickie," she called, and he checked in his course immediately and came towards her, but missing the open door, crashed into the window. "Look out, look where you're going. What's the matter with you?" cried Truda.

"I can't see you, I can't see anything. I've been struck," shouted the Major. "Oh Truda I'm blind!"

She hauled him in and he collapsed onto a chair that she pushed at him.

"Steady on old boy," she said and put a hand on his shoulder. He caught at it. "Your hands!—I thought all through those terrible trees, they kept hitting at me you see and I kept falling, but I thought if I can get back to Truda it'll be all right, her hands'll do the trick."

She stared at him: "But Dick, you know, I can't—

you know that's a con—you've known that from the beginning.''

"No, no," shouted the Major. "You can do it, Truda, you must! you can!" She tried to pull her hands away, but he caught again at both of them and thrust them against his closed eyes and held them there.

She looked down at him and for once was at a complete loss, she did not know what on earth to do, she only knew she had to do something to help her poor, poor Dick. She stopped trying to free herself and let her hands lie quietly. "Don't worry dear," she heard herself saying very firmly, "it'll be all right."

Afterwards, the next day in fact, when they were talking it over—they had been too tired to discuss it properly before—the Major said: "When you spoke, Truda, I suddenly stopped being frightened and I felt a funny tingling sort of feeling, like when you rub yourself down after a cold bath, and I knew it was OK. It was wonderful! Everybody's got to know about it, everybody!"

Truda shook her head. "No, Dickie," she said. "I don't think so, and I don't think I am going to do healing hands any more either."

"But I don't understand," spluttered the Major, "That's the best part, that's real, I know now."

"It was real that one time," said Truda slowly, "and I don't know why—perhaps because it was you. Anyway it was different and whatever you say I'm not going to do healing hands again."

"But you can't just stop. What will people think?"

"They can think what they like," said Truda, and her eyes began to brighten and open very wide. "I shall tell them my doctor says that it takes too great a toll

48

on me. Yes, he said it is too much strain at my age," she added complacently.

"You haven't got a doctor, you never have had a doctor," cried the despairing Major.

She looked at him affectionately, but pityingly. "And I won't take any more bookings," she continued. "We'll go for that holiday as soon as we can get away. I think perhaps we'll pay a long visit to Abby in the States. Better go while the going's good."

There was a pause.

"By the way," said Truda, "the milkman said the other day that they're getting on with that extension to the motorway faster than was expected."

She began to hum 'Land of Hope and Glory'. The Major sat silent until the last strains had died away, then he said: "But what shall we *do*, Truda, even if we sell up, what shall we do?"

"I'll think of something," said Truda.

THE CLOCKWORK
MOUSE

JANET RIGBY WAS TURNING out her mother's bureau, looking for the car insurance which had to be renewed. The bureau was stuffed with papers of all kinds and, not finding what she wanted, she burrowed away under them and reached into the pigeon holes. Right at the back of one of these she felt something hard and queerly shaped. She grasped it and drew it out. "Oh!" exclaimed Janet, "If it isn't the clockwork mouse—well, after all these years!" She let it fall into her lap; the key was still in its side and it looked at her with its little sharp eyes and as Janet gazed down at it, she was seven years old again and at a birthday tea with Roy. There was a cake with seven candles, and in came her mother and Aunt Hetty. Aunt Hetty was much younger than mother and had just got married to Uncle James and had been abroad and had now come to see them, and she had bought presents for the children and they were to choose. There was a splendid pencil box with a picture of a sailing ship on it, and the clockwork mouse.

"I shall choose first," said Roy, "because I am the eldest." He was only the eldest by half an hour but of course he was a boy as well and besides, said mother, someone had to choose first. Janet shut her eyes and prayed hard that he would choose the pencil box and he did. The funny little mouse had enchanted her from the moment she had seen him. She called him

Twinkle because of his bright, beady, twinkly eyes and she took him everywhere with her, including to bed though his key stuck into her rather uncomfortably. But Roy had only wanted to show off the pencil box at school and after everybody had seen and admired it, he didn't want it any more.

"Let's swop now," he said a week later, "you have the box and I'll have the mouse."

She was making a house for Twinkle out of a cardboard box. "No," she said, "I don't want to."

"Oh come on Jan," said Roy, "I'll let you play with him when I don't want him."

"No," said Janet. She caught up Twinkle and held him tightly but Roy grabbed her and she screamed.

"Now now," said mother, coming in at that moment. "What's all this about?"

"I want Jan to swop the clockwork mouse for the box, but she won't," cried Roy. "I said she could play with it just the same."

"I can't have you squabbling over Aunt Hetty's presents," said mother. "Stop crying at once Janet, give me the box and the mouse each of you. I shall take them both away for the present."

"It's not fair," sobbed Janet.

"It's perfectly fair," said mother, "I'm taking away Roy's box as well as the mouse."

"But he doesn't want the box," Janet shouted. Her mother had not answered but had walked away and, though the box had re-appeared in time if she remembered rightly, she had never seen the clockwork mouse again until this day, and tomorrow she would be forty.

Janet turned it slowly over in her lap, wound him

54

up and put him on the floor. He was a well-made mouse and ran for quite a long time. As she watched him he seemed to release in her a tide of resentment that swept over her with a force that surprised her, for she supposed she had done with all that. But the clockwork mouse unwound the years. "That's always been the way of it," she thought. There was the time when she had passed her 11+ and got into grammar school. "We can't send you to what people would say was a better school than Roy's, though I don't agree with them—but it wouldn't be fair, Janet, would it? Roy's had to spend so much time on his cricket and football, being so good at them." But Janet had overheard her father saying, "It's a pity the girl's got the brains and the boy the looks." Well, that hadn't been so bad in the end, for she had worked hard and had got her A levels and a university place to read geography. That first year at college she hadn't believed that it was possible to be so happy. Then her father had died suddenly of a heart attack. Janet looked up at the faded photograph in the silver frame on the top of the bureau. Even now she couldn't quite forgive him for dying like that. She hadn't known him very well, he seemed always in the background, but she had dimly felt he was on her side. As his photograph stared back at her, she remembered the funeral as if it were yesterday. It was in the evening when everybody had gone, except her Uncle and Aunt. Her mother, who was ill with some sort of nervous collapse, had not left her room since her father's death. They were in the sitting room when her Uncle said, "There won't be enough money I'm afraid Janet, for you to remain at college. Roy, as you know, has just started his course on business studies, and his career will take all the resources that are available; I hope to have an opening in my firm for him eventually.''

Here was a mouse worth fighting for.

"I must go back,'' she had cried, "I simply can't not go back. I can live on practically nothing, lots of people do.''

"I'm sure you don't want to be selfish, dear,'' her Aunt's voice came cooing over the years; "you heard the doctor say that your mother's heart has been affected and rest is essential for her.''

"But she won't always be like that, can't we get a nurse?''

"Quite apart from the expense,'' her Uncle had reproved, "no-one can take a daughter's place.''

"Your poor mother,'' and Aunt Hetty had begun to cry.

Janet had made one more effort later on. Her mother was better, but still advised to avoid exertion. Roy was back on vacation; it was evening after her mother had gone to bed. Aunt Hetty was staying with them and she and Roy were looking at old family photographs together. "You favour our family, Roy,'' said Aunt Hetty, "I always say so.''

"That's a great compliment, if you mean yourself, Aunt,'' said Roy. "Can't we sell this house and get a flat somewhere?'' Janet had said suddenly, "then it would be easier for mother and it would be much cheaper and perhaps I could go back to college.''

"You're a flatterer,'' said Aunt Hetty to Roy: they always flirted with each other. "What did you say, Janet?''

"I said, can't we sell this house and get a flat so that

mother could manage on her own and I could go back to college.''

Roy was outraged. ''We couldn't possibly do that. I'm not going to move into a beastly flat, thank you, and it wouldn't be fair to mother;—this is her home and it isn't as if there's any need for you to finish, Janet, I'll always take care of you.''

''I do think it would be very unwise, dear, for your mother to face a big change like that now, and rather unkind, don't you think?''

And it remained unwise and unkind for Janet to do anything but submit to what everyone thought was only her duty until it was too late. So that was that, for she had no money of her own and not much courage, and was besides, always in a muddle about what was right and what was wrong. Her mother remained something of an invalid, Janet did the shopping and most of the cooking; they had a succession of 'helps', but they were seldom very efficient. She also acted as companion and, when necessary, as nurse, and lately as secretary, for, though only in her mid-seventies, Mrs Rigby's memory was failing. They had got a car some years ago and Janet learnt to drive so that she could take her mother out. That was a sort of milestone, but after the first grim dark period was over, she couldn't really distinguish one year from another, they were like the string of dull-coloured beads that their neighbour, Mrs Jordan, always seemed to be wearing. She was an elderly, diffident, dim little woman, but useful to Janet, for she often liked to come in for a chat and a cup of coffee, which kept mother amused.

Janet picked up the mouse and dropped him into her

handbag. She really must get on with things. She found the papers she was looking for at last. The only orderly objects in the bureau were Roy's letters, which were tied up in separate packets labelled from Switzerland, from Paris, from America, for Roy, after his course was finished, had been sent abroad by his Uncle to get experience. He had not married and his objections to flats having been quite overcome, was now established in comfortable London quarters, which he shared with a friend. "A couple of old bachelors," said his mother, "but there's still plenty of time, 'a man doesn't have to hurry' is what I've always said."

The state of the bureau worried Janet—"I shall have to have a good overhaul of mother's things some time I suppose," she said to herself as she shut away the confusion, "her memory is getting worse and worse." The door bell rang. It was Mrs Jordan, and Janet's face cleared; now she could get on with baking for the birthday party tomorrow. For there was to be a dreadful party to celebrate her's and Roy's fortieth birthday. Her mother had always been a great one for parties. "Of course we must have one, as we always do," Roy had written, "Mum would be so disappointed if we didn't." "I can't make him understand that she doesn't take things in properly any more," thought Janet, exasperated. "She won't remember about our birthday, but at least it will bring him to see her, he ought really to come more often," and she had gritted her teeth and had invited Aunt Hetty and Uncle James as usual, and now she started to clean up the kitchen while Mrs Jordan chatted to her mother.

The Clockwork Mouse

"So there's to be a birthday party," said Mrs Jordan. She would have liked to have been asked, but understood it was to be only a family affair.

"Roy was such a lovely baby," said his mother, "I was so proud of him." "And of Janet too, I am sure," said Mrs Jordan. "I never bargained for a daughter," said her mother. "You've got a make-weight, the doctor said, and I own I wasn't too pleased."

"But daughters are so wonderful, what would you do without her?" said Mrs Jordan looking towards Janet, who had come into the room carrying a vase of chrysanthemums.

"Janet, you know I don't like chrysanthemums," said her mother irritably, "they always make me think of funerals."

"I'm so sorry, Mrs Rigby, I'm afraid I brought them," twittered Mrs Jordan. "I thought they'd be nice for the party."

"What party?" said Mrs Rigby.

"It was very kind, she forgets," said Janet. "Our birthday party, Mother."

"Oh yes, the birthday—Roy was such a lovely baby, I was so proud of him."

"If only she wasn't cross so often, if only she had ever really loved me, it would be bearable," thought Janet, "but now I am going to be forty tomorrow and I haven't begun,—I'll soon be as shrivelled up as Mrs Jordan."

It was nearly lunchtime before Mrs Jordan went. Janet saw her out and picked up the day's post, which she had had no time to examine before. There was a business letter for her mother, which she opened: she now passed these on to Roy if they were of any

59

financial importance. This one obviously was: it contained a cheque from a brokers for £1,000. She thrust it into her handbag for safe-keeping until she should see him, and forgot it, for there was also a card of birthday greetings from a friend. Janet had not many friends of her own age: her contemporaries were all involved with young families or jobs, and most of them had left the small provincial town where she had always lived and where there was not much going on. This card was from a college friend who had stuck by her manfully. It was quite an ordinary sort of card—a view of mountains, but for some reason Janet stared at it as though she had never known about mountains before. Their white peaks against the deepest blue annihilated the hall, the staircase, and the sound of her mother's radio. She had floated right into the picture and was dizzy with the sky, the snow and the sun. The moment passed. "How queer," thought Janet, twirling the bit of cardboard between her fingers. "Heavens the potatoes are burning!"

That night Janet dreamed of mountains. She had actually never seen one in real life—her mother preferred the sea and they went for holidays regularly to Bournemouth or Torquay. But she saw range upon range of them that night, and scaled them magnificently and with ease, and looked down from their summits over limitless sunlit spaces.

When her mother's bell, extended to her bedhead, woke her before dawn, she was seized with a violent reaction that shook her physically. She clutched at the doorway and cried, "I'll have to run away." The sober light of day gradually subdued her to despair, but she had spoken the words and although of course they could mean nothing, they refused to go, they danced around in her brain like live things. After breakfast, while tidying her room, she found herself arguing with them. ''Don't be so absurd, how could I leave Mother, I couldn't face everyone, and anyway, how on earth can I ever escape, I've no money. That ought to clinch it,'' she concluded savagely, as if to an adversary, but she found herself idiotically putting her nightdress and a toothbrush into a plastic shopping bag. ''I'm pretending: there's no harm in pretending, it's just childish and silly. If I am silly enough I'll stop being silly,'' she said. She hid the bag behind her coat in the hall and felt curiously appeased. She remembered then how once, when a child, she had read in a story instructions on how to catch a fairy. She had carried out these instructions carefully, not believing in the least that she ever would catch a fairy, yet the preparations for this gave her great satisfaction.

The morning passed with a rush; there was much to do and her mother was excited and fidgety, though why she was so she kept on forgetting.

Roy was the first to arrive for the party. He came in the family car which he had borrowed, as his own had been out of action for a short time. ''D'you know, Jan,'' he said, ''I find this old car suits me much better than mine: as Mum hardly ever goes out now and you've got the shops so near, you won't mind if I keep it for a bit, will you, of course you can always have it when you really want it.''

''Is that you Roy darling?'' called his mother from above, and he disappeared. When he came down again he said: ''Mum seems fine, I don't know why you've been making a fuss about her lately.''

61

"You never stay long enough to notice any change," said Janet, "besides she is always excited to see you."

"Yes," said Roy, "poor old Mum she doesn't get much fun, but she looks younger than ever. You said the doctor said so when he last saw her—that she might last for years."

"She *looks* all right," said Janet.

"Well, there you are then, there's nothing to worry about. There's Uncle and Aunt arriving, hope my car's not blocking their way."

"Already it's not *the* car any more," thought Janet; she said aloud: "Do you remember the birthday party when we were children, when Aunt Hetty brought the clockwork mouse?"

"Good Lord no!" said Roy hurrying to the door.

Aunt Hetty sailed into the room. She was still an attractive woman though too plump. She wore a soft pink two piece suit and pearls, and her blue-grey hair was set beautifully. She carried a bunch of roses for the birthday, and Uncle James, splendid in pin stripes, followed bearing chocolates and sherry. He wore a carnation in his button-hole. "Just as if it were a wedding," thought Janet, "but Roy always looks as if he were at a wedding,—how does he manage it?" She slipped away as soon as she could to put the last touches to the supper table; the sitting room had seemed over-full of large genial prosperous bodies.

When she came back Roy and her Uncle were talking business. "You ought to get your mother to grant you power of attorney if, as Janet says, her memory is beginning to fail," her Uncle was saying, "but she may take some persuading, old people are apt to be touchy about such things and your mother has always liked to keep things in her own hands." "Oh Mum's no problem," said Roy easily, "though it might save time I suppose, but she consults me over most things you know. By the way Janet, did you find the car insurance form and there should be a broker's cheque arriving—it'll want Mum's signature and then pay it into the bank."

"Is the dear mother resting?" enquired Aunt Hetty.

"I'll go and see if she's ready to come down," said Janet and went.

Of course, she had remembered the cheque as soon as Roy had spoken and now, as she crossed the hall, the envelope in her handbag seemed to reach out to her hidden night things behind her coat, like an electric current running along an invisible wire. "Why I could easily copy Mother's signature and write on the back 'pay Janet Rigby'. I could do that, it wouldn't be at all impossible. One thousand pounds! And when that's gone I could scrub floors if necessary. If only I could manage to get away—'over the hills and far away', over the sea, over the mountains—yes Mother I'm coming."

Her mother had had a little doze: she had not changed into the dress Janet had laid out for her and it was slow work getting her to do so and to understand and remember the reason for it. When at last she got her downstairs, Roy said: "What on earth have you been up to all this time, Jan, we're all waiting to drink healths in this excellent sherry Uncle's brought." Uncle James solemnly filled the glasses. "Speech, speech," cried Aunt Hetty. "Oh no!" said Janet, but Roy enjoyed making speeches.

"On behalf of Janet and myself," he began. "But all the tunes that she could play," sang Janet to herself, "was over the hills and far away," and she heard no more till the finish.—"How lucky we are to be able to celebrate in this dear old home and now I want to propose another health—to our dear mother, long life to her."

"Darling Roy," said Mrs Rigby, "but is it my birthday? I really hadn't remembered." "Supper's ready," said Janet and they went into the dining room.

"What a lovely cake, Janet," said Aunt Hetty, "and what a splendid spread you've provided. Isn't it a marvellous satisfaction to feed the family, dear, I've always found it so."

"Better look out though Roy," said his Uncle, "you're putting on weight a bit, take warning by me, my boy."

"Well I've decided to take a ski-ing holiday in Austria this winter, that ought to help."

"That's a very good idea Roy," said Aunt Hetty, "though I like a man to be well covered myself."

"Like to like," thought Janet. "Over the sea, over the mountains. I shall have to go while they are still here, I couldn't leave Mother alone in the house, but nor can they. That means I'll have to go this night— this very night." She knew for a certainty that if she did not act at once she would never do so.

"I'd have liked to have tried ski-ing myself," said Uncle James, "but I'm past that now. I didn't make hay while the sun shone, always thought I was indispensable. No one is indispensable. Remember that, it's the truth."

"The car key is in the hall, but how on earth can I manage to escape without notice?" thought Janet. She felt in her handbag, which was in her

The Clockwork Mouse

lap beneath the table, for reassurance that the cheque was still there, and her fingers closed upon the clockwork mouse,—she had forgotten he was there too, nestling beside the cheque.

"Janet, you're not eating anything," said Aunt Hetty, "there's no need for *you* to starve, you're looking quite scraggy."

Janet helped herself to cake with one hand and with the other felt again in her bag—the skin on the top of her head began to tingle with excitement.

"It looks like a birthday cake," said her mother. "Is it somebody's birthday? But there aren't any candles."

"Perhaps forty candles seemed too many, eh Janet?" said her Uncle. Janet took a large bite of cake and began to wind up the mouse inside her bag.

"I was sorry to hear you'd had an accident with your car, Roy," said Aunt Hetty and they all began to talk about cars.

Janet bent down and put the clockwork mouse on the floor: he began to run, Aunt Hetty shrieked and everyone jumped up. All eyes were riveted on the mouse and Janet slipped from the room, caught up her coat, her bag and the car key and rushed from the house. The good old car started up immediately and she drove off as fast as she could go into the night.

"Tom, Tom, the piper's son, stole a pig and away did run," sang Janet. "Roy can have the clockwork mouse at last, he and Mother can play with it together."

RED BEARDS

THE OLD BATTERED CAR drew to a halt and the man crouched over the wheel, relaxed and let his arms drop loosely down. He had been driving all day without a stop for food and suddenly had felt exhausted and, besides, he had lost his way. He had left the motorway because of a traffic block and was in a winding lane between fields, and there were no signposts and no village in sight, only a nearby cottage. "I'll ask the way to the nearest pub," he said to himself. "I must get a drink and a bit of food inside me before I go on."

It was toward the end of a cold March day; the north wind had piled up heavy clouds but between them were clear spaces and the setting sun broke through and lit up the old red brick of the cottage so that it glowed against the dark grey of the banking clouds. The man, stumbling up the little brick path, was almost dazzled by the reflected light from the windows. He knocked on the door and it was opened by a little red-haired boy of about seven or eight years old who stared up at him with wide eyes and then before he could speak, shouted out back into the house, "Mum, Mum, it's Uncle at last!" A plump middle-aged woman came out of a side door and peered at him. Looking in from the now dim cold garden, he could see the anxious expression on her face give place to a smile of welcome. "Why Ben," she said, "you did get my letter then. I *am* glad. We didn't want to advertise, that might have caused trouble, and I'd just about given you up. Come in, come in, don't stand there in the cold. I felt sure my letter 'd bring you if it ever got to you." She didn't wait for an answer, but threw the room door open behind her and he followed her over the threshold. The little boy sprang to shut out the wind and the dark. An open fire was burning brightly and there was a lamp with a red shade and a table set with plates and mugs, and in the room was a smell of fried bacon. This was all the man noticed at first, but it was very noticeable to him for he was hungry and cold, so he stood there saying nothing. The warmth and the smell of food and the surprise of the greeting had bemused him. "They've mistaken me in the dark for someone else," he thought, "they'll find out in a minute and then I'll ask the way."

While he waited for the woman to speak, his eyes dwelt on the loaded table. "I only wish I *was* the chap," he said to himself.

"Did you have much trouble finding the way? I see you've managed to get hold of a car—there's no other means of getting here now. I did my best to tell you—it's a bit tricky, but I thought you'd have your head screwed on the right way. Bob always said you were the clever one. You've been clever enough to get here just in time for supper," she laughed, "you must've had a long day of it, sit down now and have it while it's hot, you can see to the car and your things afterwards." She pulled up an old wooden armchair with a cushion and he sank down on it. "Thanks ever so," he said and thought, "I must have dropped off in the car, I hope I don't wake up till I've eaten something."

Red Beards

The woman piled up his plate and poured out tea and, as he ate and drank, a deep sense of comfort invaded him, all the more powerful because of the unreality, in which the room with its leaping fire light (to which he was quite unaccustomed), the bright china, the little boy and the round-faced, dark-eyed woman all swam before his eyes in a haze.

They talked hardly at all during the meal. The woman asked a few questions about the journey, whether the traffic had been heavy, what the weather had been like, what sort of car had he got and he had answered her briefly, and the little boy had gazed at him silently. At last he pushed back his chair and mechanically pulled out his pipe. "That's good," said the woman approvingly, "I like a man to smoke a pipe, I've missed it ever since Bob went. You must be tired out, we can talk tomorrow; I wrote as soon as I could, you know, after your Dad died; but I'll leave you in peace to smoke your pipe. Johnny stop staring at your Uncle and give me a hand with the supper things."

"I must tell her she's made a mistake as soon as she comes back," thought the man. But he still felt in a dream, no longer in charge of events, so that when Johnny ran in and cried: "I'm to show you where to put your car," he got up without speaking and followed him out into the lane.

The importance of acting as a guide quite overcame the little boy's shyness and he began to chat. "Your car's rather old isn't it?"

"Yes," said the man, "it is old but it still goes."

"My Dad had a car, but I was little then so I can't remember it. Will you take me in yours tomorrow? We might go fishing. Look, here's where to put your car—

71

in here." He opened a gate into a field and the man backed the car into it. "Are you OK?" shouted the boy. "OK is it?" the man said to himself and sat motionless in the seat. "Didn't you hear, Uncle? Shall I shut the gate?" shouted the little boy again.

"Yes I heard," shouted the man back, "OK it is!" He took a shabby case out of the car and banged its door. The boy put his hand into his and they went back into the cottage out of the cold and dark. "He's a nice little tyke," thought the man. He'd have liked a boy of his own, but Tracy wasn't for having a child at any price.

"I'll show you where you're to sleep," said Johnny and led the way up a narrow staircase to a bedroom almost filled by a big old iron double bed with a patchwork quilt. There was a chest of drawers opposite with a framed photograph on it.

"That's my Dad," said Johnny, "and that's you." The man sat down suddenly on the bed, dropping his case, but the little boy seized the photograph and brought it to him. "That's how I knew you, your beard is longer now though you haven't got so much hair on your head and you're thinner, but of course you're older, but I knew your beard was red like my hair because my Grandad always said you was the red Devil and my Dad was the black one."

The man peered at the photograph of the two men. Yes it was like, it could have been taken for himself when younger—the nose short and snub like his, the forehead rather low and broad, the mouth hidden of course by the beard. The width of shoulders and the height were similar too, but the set of the head was quite different, it was side-cocked and looked out at him with a cheerful self-confidence.

"Johnny, Johnny," called the woman's voice from below, "leave your Uncle now and get to bed."

Left alone, the man slowly replaced the photograph on the chest. "It's a rum go," he muttered, "but I could just about do with a free night's sleep in a good bed. In the morning I'll slip away before anyone's about."

The woman wasn't surprised at his turning in early.

"You look done for," she said kindly. Later, under the heavy, warm quilt, he could not sleep at first because of the strangeness of the big bed. He had never experienced such a bed before. He stretched out his legs and touched the cold edges of the huge mattress and drew them in again quickly to the warmth of his body—yes it *was* still his body, though everything else was so different from the place he had left behind and the place he was making for in the vague hope of a job. At last he slept and so soundly that he did not stir till long after he had intended. He lay for some moments, wondering where on earth he was. There was sun streaming in at the low window and voices below, a woman's voice and, at the sound, it all came back to him and he sat up in bed to listen. There was a clink of milk bottles and the woman's voice again: "I want an extra pint today Bill, I told you I was expecting my Bob's brother from Canada. Well he came last night, I thought he'd come and not write, there's a bit of money waiting for him, you see, from his Dad." Then a man's voice, "What's he like then, Mrs Bowers?"

"Quiet like, though I've always heard he was a bit wild and a rolling stone, but of course he's older now. I only met him once years and years ago at my wedding. Johnny's taken to him."

"Will he be staying long?"

"I don't know. I hope he won't be off at once anyways. I like a bit of company. I miss my shop, you know."

A knock came at the bedroom door, it opened gently and the little boy sidled in.

"I've had my breakfast and I've got to catch the bus for school. Can we go out in your car when I get home?"

"OK," said the man, and the child disappeared.

"So there's a bit of money waiting," he said to himself. "Well, as I'm still here perhaps I'll have a bite of breakfast before I go."

The room downstairs was full of sunlight, and the woman, Mrs Bowers, was tidying up the hearth. "Hullo Ben," she said, "I let you have your sleep out and you looked as though you needed it. I'll bring you your breakfast in a tick." The man sat down in the same cushioned chair, already it seemed to him to be *his* chair. He couldn't remember when he had last had a proper breakfast, certainly never one brought to him. He generally got himself a cup of Ness and a slice of bread and marge while Tracy was sleeping it off, and since she had walked out on him he hadn't often even bothered to do that. Now Mrs Bowers carried in a couple of eggs and a plate of buttered toast and a blue and white teapot and jug. While he was eating she got the fire going, but when he had finished she took a paper from an old bureau in the corner and sat down at the table.

"I told you in my letter that your Dad went off peaceful; well they do, don't they, at that age. I'd fetched him here of course, wasn't going to have him

74

put in a Home, but he left all his affairs shipshape and here's a copy of the Will for you to see. Becaue he didn't know where you might be, you having no settled home, he made me executor, but your share's here in the Bank for the asking and I can make it over to you right away.'' The man took the paper she pushed across to him and read it. It was very short and simple: everything was left "between my son Benjamin Bowers and my daughter-in-law Mary Bowers in trust for my grandson, John Robert Bowers'', and there was a separate sum of money to the said Mary Bowers as executor. He sat looking at the paper without speaking.

"I expect you feel bad at not seeing your Dad before he went,'' she said, "now you just smoke your pipe while I get on with my jobs and do my bit of shopping.''

"Handed to me on a plate,'' said the man to himself after she had left him, "but I reckon it's too risky, besides I've always kept pretty straight, meant to anyway. Yet it's the first bit of luck I've ever had and just handed over to me, a tidy sum too.''

He sat on staring at the piece of paper on the table. In spite of his night's sleep he still felt tired and unwilling to move or think. It was so peaceful there by the fire. When Mary Bowers came bustling back he muttered his thanks.

"We didn't know where you were,'' she said again, half apologetically, "that's why I had to see to things.''

"Of course,'' said the man.

"After Bob died it was a lovely letter you wrote me, I got it still. Then I didn't hear again till the card last Christmas from Canada, so that was where I wrote. It's strange how things turn out—Bob, who always was the stay-at-home, goes off sudden with his heart, serving in the shop one morning, and you, who've been half round the world and in all sorts of tight corners are safe and sound still, though you don't look too well I must say—you're much too thin for a man of your size, Ben.''

''I've been ill,'' he said—that at least was true.

''Well I'm a good cook, though I say it myself and I'll soon have some flesh on you and I'm really glad to have a man to feed again. I've missed Bob so, that's why I came back here where I'm known—I was brought up here and I didn't want to stay up north without Bob or the shop. Now, about the money—Mr Lewis at the Bank, he's a friendly man, known me for years has Mr Lewis. He's just waiting for you to turn up. I told him I didn't know quite where you were, but I'd written to the last address. I was beginning to wonder, but you didn't get away at once, did you?''

''No,'' said the man: then he added slowly, ''this illness it's made me forget things.''

She gave him a quick glance. ''What a shame,'' she said, ''but don't you worry, you need a rest that's all.'' Then the boy came rushing in from school, it was a half holiday.

''Can we go fishing? We can get to the river in the car,'' he cried.

''You mustn't bother your Uncle,'' said his mother.

''Women can't fish can they?'' said the boy. He put a hand on the man's knee. ''I'm so glad you're here,'' he said.

''OK, OK,'' said the man, ''you show me,'' and they went out together.

And the day passed and in the evening the man was

still there and at night went up to the big bed again. But before he lay down on it he examined the room more carefully. There were a few books on a shelf in a corner. He took them out one by one, not looking at the titles, but at the fly leaves, and on one he found what he was looking for: a name, "Ben Bowers" written in a bold round script. "Of course it might not be his writing, but I bet it is," he said. He did not know why he was so certain. He found an unpaid bill in his pocket and copied the signature several times till he got it fairly like. The photograph on the chest of drawers watched him. He began arguing with it.

"Well, if you don't turn up soon it'll be your fault. I don't say that I'll take any of the money, I may just slip away d'you hear? All I say is that if you were in my shoes you'd understand. But you've never been in my shoes, not by a long chalk. I've never had your luck, never had a family, see? not to speak of anyway, and now I'm about finished and done with. I've lost my job, I've lost my girl, I've lost about everything but the old car. 'What's that to you?' you're saying. Well I didn't ask to come here, did I? I was only wanting to know the way. London, that's where I was making for, so now you know." He turned away from the smiling face and rolled under the quilt.

A week passed and the man had not gone. He had drawn out a moderate sum from the Bank. "Well, it was expected of me," he told the photograph. There had been no trouble about this (Mrs Bowers was well known and respected) and he had bought Johnny a new fishing rod and some clothes for himself, and had filled up his petrol tank, and there was nothing to wait for but discovery, and yet he stayed on. Every night he said, "I'll go tomorrow," but he did not go. The days flowed on so easily and pleasantly. He got the garden tidy. "When the grass is done there's the potato patch to dig," Mary said. "I don't know anything about gardening really," he said doubtfully. "Never stayed long enough anywhere I expect," she said, "Well it's never too late to learn," and he found he liked it.

"What did you want with rushing around the world?" he said to Ben that night, "when you could have settled down with your family?—bought a little shop, perhaps, with a garden."

In the evenings Mary and he would look at the telly together or chat. The man heard a lot about Bob and Ben and their Dad. "Luckily," he thought, "she likes talking better than listening." Most people, he discovered, were not much interested in anything outside their own particular world. But he spent a day in the Public Library of the neighbouring town, looking up articles on Canada in the Encyclopedia. "Uncle Ben's fished from icebergs and seen bears in the Rockies," boasted Johnny.

At the end of the third week, one afternoon, he was in the back garden finishing off some digging when Johnny came running round the corner of the house and there was something in the child's look that made him exclaim, "What's up then?"

"There's someone at the gate asking for Mum, he says it's very particular. I told him Mum wasn't in, she's gone to the village and he asked if anyone was at home. I said my Uncle was and he laughed and said well he was another Uncle and that was a silly sort of joke, wasn't it? I don't think he's very well, he couldn't

walk properly. I think perhaps he's drunk. I didn't like
him.''

''I'll see to him,'' said the man quickly, ''and now
you be off indoors and stay there till I come.'' It was
the first time he had spoken authoritatively to the little
boy and he obeyed at once. To himself the man said:
''So he's here at last, well he can wait now till I've
done.'' He finished the row of digging, even scraping
the spade and putting it away. Then he went slowly
towards the lane.

At first he could see nobody, then he made him
out—a huddled figure half-sitting, half-lying under the
hedge. An old cap had fallen sideways over his face
and he was snoring. ''The boy's dead right, he's as
drunk as a lord.'' He went nearer and peered down:
what he could see of the face was disfigured by a
recent-looking scar, the hair at the edges of the cap was
grey and the beard too was grey and scanty. ''It could
have been red once,'' thought the man. He bent over
and very gently began to feel in the uppermost pocket
of the coat. There was only some loose cash there but,
as the snoring continued unabated, he slipped his hand
underneath and out of an inside pocket, from which
it was protruding, brought a worn leather pocket-book.
It contained a letter and a passport. The name on both
these was Benjamin Bowers. The passport photograph
was recognizable and the letter was from Mary
announcing old Mr Bowers' death.

''So you're Ben,'' said the man aloud, then a sudden
rage possessed him that, after all, Ben should turn out
to be a drunken sot who had wasted all his chances.
He seized him by the shoulders and shook him
furiously. The old cap fell into the ditch and the face

that met his froze from blank surprise to horror. A choked cry broke out: "Bloody Hell! it's Ben—but I left you dead and cold on the road and the bloody car smashed up over you. I thought I was a goner too, with my face torn to bits. It wasn't my fault, mate—who said I'd had too much? I swear you was dead and cold, Ben, before I came to and before I took anything from you. I done you no harm, you didn't need your ticket any more. You wouldn't grudge me that ticket home, mate—you knew as how I was needing to get away out of the country—I never read the letter about the money till after, I swear it. I didn't mean any harm coming here, I was only curious to see how things was." The hoarse voice died away and then almost at once started up again shrilly. "I left you dead, I say—you're not bloody real—it's the drink, it's only the drink."

The two men stared at each other a moment in silence and then one of them threw back his head and roared with laughter; he hadn't laughed like that for years. "That makes two of us," he shouted, "you're no more Ben Bowers than I am,—less, much less, for I'm known here, see, and now I've got the proof." He waved the letter and the passport above his head. "D'you understand? It's no good, you be off and if you show your face here ever again I'll set the police on you." He bent down, picked up the old cap and threw it at the shambling figure that, without a word of reply, turned and staggered off down the lane. Then he opened the gate and ran up the little brick path, *home* . . .

THE VIEW

MISS HILDA PRITCHARD'S garden was shut in by neighbouring houses, except for one gap through which she got a view of Beech Hill, rising to the east of the village, crowned splendidly with a big clump of the trees from which it took its name.

Hilda loved this view. When she and her brother first came to live at "Beechview" (as they proudly renamed their new home: it had simply been No. 23 High Street before), they had built a little summer house in the garden, from which you could look first across the lawn and the flower borders and then, beyond the cluster of roofs through the gap up, triumphantly, to the view. Since her brother had died and she had begun to feel a bit old and lonely, and not able to get about so much, her view had become even more precious to Hilda Pritchard. It was a sort of company and she was proud of it too. Sometimes she would ask a less fortunate neighbour to enjoy a cup of tea and her view in the summer house. It was pleasant to feel that the poor soul had no such bonus and to hear it enviously admired.

At the beginning of August, however, Hilda went to stay with a friend at Bexhill. She admired this friend, Miss Armorel Pike, very much: she was such an interesting person. She had studied astrology and anthropology and knew many fascinating things about primitive tribes and their sometimes rather horrid customs. Hilda often said she ought to give a talk on

T.V., or at least on radio. They had met on a package tour to Haiti, and Armorel had told her much about the native inhabitants not known to the ordinary traveller—but of course everything was being spoilt now by tourists. Going to stay with Armorel was almost as good as going on several tours. In the guest room there were rugs from Mexico and a carved walrus ivory box made by Eskimos and a bedcover from Nigeria.

Hilda was all the more pleased to pay this visit because she had decided she really must have Beechview repainted this summer and she hoped to get this done while she was away. Not that this was very likely, she admitted to herself. Every job seemed to take longer and longer these days and Tom Pettey was a lazy, easygoing man. But he was employed throughout the village and had always done work for her and her brother. Armorel said that the position of the stars was propitious for all new building enterprises just now. Hilda wondered if painting Beechview could count as new building enterprise, but she had decided to have the front door blue instead of its former black so perhaps it would. She intended to return before the bank holiday to avoid the crowds. Three weeks away was quite enough time to be in someone else's house and Armorel's, though interesting, was rather chilly on wet days and too full of matting.

She enjoyed herself though. Armorel took her to a good lecture: on the Yanomami Indians, with splendid slides and a most intriguing talk on the Evil Eye—it was quite extraordinary how this seemed to work among all primitive peoples. ''There are more things in Heaven and Earth than are dreamed of'', quoted Armorel.

When Hilda got home she was annoyed, though not

surprised, to find that Tom had only finished the front and one side of the house. The blue door looked very nice, however, and the front garden was welcoming and bright with late summer flowers; the stocks and antirrhinums had done especially well that year. She thought she would not bother to unpack yet but would take a tea tray out to the summerhouse. She wondered if the beeches had begun to turn; no, it was a little too early, she decided. She made the tea and allowed herself two chocolate biscuits to celebrate her homecoming. After all she was sure she had lost some weight at Armorel's, whose diet was very pure and herbal. She carried out the tray carefully, which was just as well, as Tom had left his ladder lying on the lawn in front of the summer house. She put the tray down on the table, sank thankfully into her favourite garden chair and, full of loving anticipation, looked up at her view. She could not believe what met her eyes. There was no view, it had vanished! Instead she saw a hideous scaffolding protruding from the back of Lavender Cottage which completely blocked the gap that had been so precious, so invaluable. Hilda felt her heart thumping quite violently; she was given to palpitations when agitated. Her hand trembled so much that the cup of hot tea she was holding spilt itself all down her best skirt and soaked through, but she never felt this or even noticed it spilling. She put the cup down and rose unsteadily to her feet.

Just then Tom Pettey appeared round the corner of the house. "Knew you'd be home again Miss Pritchard," he said, "thought I'd look in and see how you liked your door. I'm taking our Bessie to her Gran's tomorrow and 'twon't be worth starting work after that.

I'll be here Friday perhaps and then it'll be the holiday weekend.''

Hilda took no notice of what he was saying.

"Tom, what's going on here?" she asked.

Tom turned round slowly. "Oh that," he said, "it's them new people, them Purvises, they're putting on an extension to Lavender Cottage, got a town firm to do it, local labour's not good enough for them seems."

"It must be stopped," said Hilda.

Tom looked surprised and gratified, but shook his head. "Can't be done Miss Pritchard, people can have who they like to work for them, within reason that is."

"Oh I didn't mean that!" exclaimed Hilda, "I mean the whole thing must be stopped immediately." Her voice sounded shrilly.

Tom kicked the ladder at his feet. "Well that can't be done neither. They've got permission from the Council all right, no one objected, the notice was put up quite proper, though inconspicious like, on the side fence."

"I never saw it. Why did no one tell me, it must have gone up before I went away," said Hilda furiously.

"I suppose no one thought it'd do no harm to no one," said Tom.

"But it does to me," wailed Hilda, "it's taken away my view."

Tom turned slowly round again, "So it does, that's a pity that is, but it can't be helped now though, once it's started, for a view's not legal objection I'm thinking."

Hilda did not speak so he went on: "Well, I'll be getting along now, I just looked in for a word. I'll be finishing your job back part of next week then Miss Pritchard, if it keeps fine."

He disappeared and Hilda went in and rang her solicitor who confirmed the information that the loss of a view was no legal cause for complaint.

"But I shall complain all the same," said Hilda to herself, "I'll call and make a personal appeal; they can't realize what they are doing to me." She decided to put this off till the next morning for the workmen had gone home, so no more of their devilish business could be carried on that evening and what with her journey and the shock, she felt quite worn out. She spent a miserable night.

The following day her help, Mrs Bunch, arrived. "Morning Miss Pritchard," she said, "did you have a good holiday?"

"Mrs Bunch did you know about this terrible extension they're having put up at Lavender Cottage?" demanded Hilda. She could not bear to talk about anything else.

"I couldn't help but know," said Mrs Bunch, "for my cousin's girl she does for Mrs Purvis, such a dust and dirt she says coming in through the windows and under the doors, be they never so tight shut, and the racket something dreadful. That's not very nice for Miss Pritchard to come home to next to her garden, I said,— never mind dear, it'll soon be over and done with, those workmen are ever so quick, not like some I know." Mrs Bunch, who had also worked a long while for Hilda, disapproved of Tom on principle.

"It's not that," said Hilda, "it's my view, oh Mrs Bunch my view is quite blocked up."

Mrs Bunch made a clicking noise with her top plate, which didn't fit very well, but this she found useful for emphasis. "Think of that, and I know what store you sets by that view, that's a downright shame that is."

"It's not right," said Hilda, "people ought not to be able to do such a thing, but they can it seems."

"I don't know why they should want a lot more rooms to clean I'm sure," said Mrs Bunch, "just the two of them. *She* don't want it, says it'll spoil the garen. They've had words about it my cousin's girl says, but he wins. He's one as always gets his own way and what's worse, my cousin's girl says, he gets it for your own good, never at a loss he is, says it's all for her so as she can give her parties and see her friends so as he won't be under her feet. She says she don't want no parties, but it's no manner of use her talking."

"I'm going round there this morning to complain," said Hilda. Mrs Bunch shook her head to signify doubt and dismay, but began to hum the cheerful little tuneless hum with which she always accompanied her work. She was sorry for Miss Pritchard, but that is different from being sorry for oneself, besides she relished anything in the shape of drama.

There were two large cars parked in front of Lavender Cottage. Hilda negotiated these with difficulty and pushed open the gate. Immediately she was assailed by a nasty little terrier who yapped and snarled round her feet. Trembling with annoyance and fear she pressed the bell. Mr Purvis opened the door. He was a large florid man with a jovial manner. "Come right in," he shouted above the din of the dog, "don't mind him, that's his welcome, that is, pleased to see you I'm sure."

Hilda edged into the house.

"I live at Beechview," she began.

"I know, I know and a very nice house it is too." He put an arm round Hilda and propelled her into a sitting room where Mrs Purvis, a pale small blonde, was seated before the television. She did not turn it off.

"Here's our good neighbour come to call, Elsie," said Mr Purvis.

"Hullo," said Mrs Purvis, throwing her a side glance, "do sit down."

Hilda sat on the edge of the nearest chair.

"A very nice house, Beechview," shouted Mr Purvis, "but a bit on the large size for you isn't it? We ought to have done an exchange, that's what." He laughed immoderately. "We fell in love with this cottage when we saw it, but it's too small. I'm a large man, you see." He laughed again.

Hilda did not feel in the least like laughing, how dare he suggest that her house was too big for her!

"Mr Purvis," she began.

"Victor please," he said, "and Elsie," he added. "Let me give you a glass of sherry m'dear."

"No thank you," said Hilda.

Mr Purvis took no notice, "Always good for you, sherry," he said advancing towards her with a full glass, so that she had to accept it, but she was determined not to drink any. There was no table near so she sat with it uncomfortably in her hand. The terrier was still sniffing suspiciously at her ankles.

"Now what can I do for you?" asked Mr Purvis.

"It's about that extension you're building," said Hilda.

"The noise," he said soothingly, "I know, but it's worse for us if that's any comfort, and I promise you m'dear it'll soon be over. The noisier the quicker, we tell ourselves, don't we Elsie. They're a jolly good firm, go at it with all their guts, not like some of these locals."

"It's not the noise," said Hilda, "it's my view, your extension will blot out my view."

"Oh ho! Oh ho!" said Mr Purvis, "if that isn't bad luck, very sorry but it can't be helped, can it. So there was a view, was there, shouldn't have thought it."

"Yes," said Hilda with a rush, "between the gap in the houses, a beautiful view of Beech Hill and I was wondering if you could possibly see your way to lowering the roof, the roof of your extension I mean, or of building on the other side, over the garage perhaps. I don't want to complain, but—"

"No use if you did want to," cut in Mr Purvis, "a view's not private property or ancient lights m'dear." He gave another of his large genial laughs.

Hearing it, Hilda knew there was no hope, no possible use in saying any more, but Mr Purvis now leant towards her confidentially. "Take my word for it, m'dear, after a little while you won't miss it; what's more, didn't the east wind blow through that gap like nobody's business; there's nothing like a gap between buildings to put an edge to a wind. You'll be far more cosy when it's filled up."

"I don't want to be cosy," Hilda said, "I want my view." She set the sherry glass down on the carpet where it was promptly overturned by the terrier, and stood up.

"Oh must you go," murmured Mrs Purvis.

"I'm afraid I must," said Hilda, "Goodbye and please don't trouble to see me out." But Victor was at the front door before her.

"That's OK then," he said beaming, "so glad you called."

"I was a fool to go," said Hilda furiously to herself

as she stumbled home past the parked cars. She relieved
her feelings a little that evening by writing a long letter
to Armorel and, as she was doing this, she suddenly
thought of that talk on the Evil Eye and the way it
seemed to work among those Yanomami Indians. It had
sounded so convincing. "I'm too tired now," she
thought, but tomorrow I believe I'll give it a trial.
Armorel said there's no knowing what concentrated
waves of love or hate will do."

So all next day she stayed at home, missing the W.I.
afternoon meeting and doing her best with waves
directed towards Victor Purvis. She found it very hard
work. For one thing she had no very clear idea what
actually to have in mind for Mr Purvis, other than some
misfortune or other to make him stop the work, and this
was perhaps too vague. She was certain that this sort
of thing needed practice, especially for a Westerner. It
was all very well for Armorel to talk, but had she ever
tried it? Hilda was pretty certain that she had not. She
herself ended up with a bad headache, which was not
improved when, on opening the window for some fresh
air, she saw Victor swinging down the road to post a
letter. He was whistling 'Rule Britannia' loudly and
looked distressingly healthy.

This was Friday and, after lunch, Tom turned up to
put in an afternoon's work. He knocked off a bit early
because it was the holiday weekend and came to report
to Hilda as she was in the kitchen, putting on her kettle
for tea which she could no longer bear to carry out to
the summer house.

"I'll be leaving my ladder here, Miss Pritchard," said
Tom, "wouldn't do it much good loading it on and off
my van when not needed—it's feeling its age see—I

must get down to repairing it one of these days, joint's gone in one place, it takes me all right still, though, if I mind and don't put on any more weight," he chuckled. "I've moved it off your grass to your front path, so it won't make no mark."

"Oh yes, thank you," said Hilda; the kettle had just boiled and she was filling her pot, wondering whether she should offer him a cup, but deciding against it as her head was still troubling her and she wanted to be left alone. The men working on the extension did not stop till long after Tom's departure and the noise of the hammering and of their blaring transistors nearly drove her mad. When they packed up she took two aspirins and went to bed early.

The weather broke in time for the holiday. Great black clouds rolled up from the north, though no rain fell at once. Hilda, however, decided against going out and just before lunch she had a visitor. It was Mr Purvis. His bulk towered above her as he stood on the doorstep beaming. "Hilda," he said, "it *is* Hilda isn't it? Elsie said she was sure it was—well, m'dear we're in a bit of a fix. There's a storm brewing, as I'm sure you can see, I felt a drop or two as a matter of fact just now, and those damned workmen (sorry m'dear) they've left the tarpaulin loose and there's a gap where they had to knock a bit of the old roof away, just over our bedroom, believe it or not! Now I happened to see a ladder on your front path, having a bit of painting done aren't you? and thought to myself if that little lady'll let me borrow that ladder I can get that cover fixed up. They've taken away all their ladders and we've only got a step."

"Well," said Hilda, "I don't know I'm sure."

"It's quite a lucky chance, I said to Elsie," went on

The View

Mr Purvis, taking no notice of her hesitation, "Hilda having that ladder there." There was a little pause. "Very well then," said Hilda nodding, "it does seem sort of lucky, doesn't it."

She watched him taking the long ladder away then and there. He was such a big strong man, it seemed to cost him no effort.

It began to rain in good earnest soon after lunch and Hilda went round shutting all her windows. She forgot to drink the cup of tea she had poured for herself, she also forgot to bring in her washing until it was too late and it was drenched. "Dear, dear, how forgetful I am growing," she said to herself, "but it's no use worrying." She listened to the rain pattering down and switched on her fire for she felt quite chill. Presently there was another sound besides the rain, she could just hear it—shrill and very rapidly increasing—like a police car or an ambulance rushing past. "I'm glad I shut the windows," Hilda thought, "that sort of noise always makes me feel funny."

It rained steadily all that day, but the next morning it was better and Hilda decided to go for a walk. She took the path that led in the opposite direction from Lavender Cottage. It skirted a field and led eventually to the church and was generally pretty unfrequented, but today though, as she came round through the churchyard she saw that there was quite a little group of people at the gate of the Vicarage. One of them was the Vicar who, when he saw her, detached himself and came to meet her.

"Good morning Vicar," said Hilda. But instead of greeting her in his usual cheerful way, he looked very grave.

"Good morning Miss Pritchard," he said, "have you heard our sad news? No I can see you have not, and I am afraid it may come as a great shock, as it has to us all—your neighbour, Mr Purvis, had a bad fall yesterday—they took him to hospital, but it was all over before they got there—I am just on my way now to see his poor wife."

"Oh dear!" exclaimed Hilda, "how terrible."

"You have gone quite pale," said the Vicar solicitously, "you had better go home and rest, I will see you to your door."

"It was the ladder, Vicar," sobbed Elsie Purvis, "he was trying to fix the tarpaulin—the ladder, the top part slipped somehow and it's hard paving below. Victor wasn't a careless man," she went on between her sobs, "quite the reverse, he never never had accidents, it was the ladder, it wasn't ours you see," (usually it was Victor who had done the talking, but now Elsie didn't seem able to stop) "—he'd borrowed it from Beechview, she was having her painting done, it was left there and he borrowed it, you never know do you?"

"Yes, yes," interposed the Vicar, "I see, I see, a very sad accident, a terrible thing to have happened." "Dear, dear," he thought to himself, "no wonder Miss Pritchard looked pale, but of course she mustn't be allowed to blame herself—it must have been Tom Pettey's ladder, getting old and a bit careless I fear, but *he* couldn't have known that anyone was going to borrow it—he'll get into trouble over this, poor chap." The Vicar was a kindly man and fond of his parishioners.

Hilda had taken a couple more aspirins when she had got home. She felt another headache coming on from trying not to remember that she had forgotten something. She tried instead to recollect what Armorel had taught her about Yoga and relaxation, but she could not do this clearly enough to help. "The trouble with me is that I don't pay enough attention to what people say and that's why I forget so easily, though you can't properly call it forgetting, can you, when you have never really heard it." This conclusion reached, she felt better and her headache receded, in fact after a while she found herself quite cheerful.

She ordered some flowers for the funeral, nothing ostentatious, of course, just a nice spray, but she decided against attending. Funerals, like ambulances, always made her feel funny. Besides really he hadn't been a very nice man.

"Didn't you go then?" said Mrs Bunch, surprised. "It was a lovely funeral, pity to miss it. Mrs Purvis' wreath was something out of this world, must've cost a fortune. Well, what's meant to be *is* meant to be, that's what I always think, and it's no use to take on, though that's not to say Tom's not worried about that there ladder. Shouldn't wonder if there's an inquest," she added with relish. In the event there seemed however to be really no case for an inquest. Tom bought himself a new ladder, but he did not start work again at once, and Hilda did not send for him. It was natural that he should be a bit upset, she thought, and anyway I don't want him bothering round for a little. He and Mrs Bunch never stop talking and there's no denying that I'm getting a bit deaf, it's a strain listening to them. He'll finish my painting all right before winter comes."

There was no work being done at Lavender Cottage either.

"Mrs Bunch," remarked Hilda one day, "I remember you saying that Mrs Purvis never wanted that extension built, so I suppose they'll soon be taking the scaffolding away." Mrs Bunch put down the hoover she was just bringing into the sitting room. "Well now," she said, "you can never tell with people can you. My cousin's girl she always said, like I told you, as how the Purvises were cat and dog together and the dog getting the best of it—'cording to her she's better off without him, though that's not a nice way to talk now I tell her. But, would you believe it, she says that he might have been the Pope and the Prince of Wales rolled into one the way she goes on now about him, (got her own way of putting things that girl, always has). Anyways, she says as how he was so sold on that extension and sacrificed his life for it even, in a manner of speaking you might say, so that she's going to make it a sort of memorial to him and move all his pictures and photos and his favourite chair and his books and his golf clubs and all into it, like Queen Victoria did Prince Albert's—she reads a lot does my cousin's girl, you wouldn't believe."

"But the work's stopped," cried Hilda.

"Only temporary, the men knocked off for the funeral week and to fill in time they started on another job, see. But they'll be back again soon, my cousin's girl says, and the same dirt and dust to cope with, something shocking."

There was no response, and when Mrs Bunch had plugged in the hoover, she looked round and found herself alone.